THE BEAUTIFUL BUTTERFLY

A FOLKTALE FROM SPAIN

RETOLD BY *Judy Sierra*

ILLUSTRATED BY *Victoria Chess*

Clarion Books ❧ *New York*

CLARION BOOKS
a Houghton Mifflin Company imprint
215 Park Avenue South, New York, NY 10003
Text copyright © 2000 by Judy Sierra
Illustrations copyright © 2000 by Victoria Chess

The type for this book was set in 14-point Kennerly.
Illustrations were executed in gouache and sepia pen and ink.
Book design by Sylvia Frezzolini Severance.

Printed in Singapore.

LIBRARY OF CONGRESS CATALOGING-IN-PUBLICATION DATA

Sierra, Judy.
The beautiful butterfly : a folktale from Spain /
retold by Judy Sierra ; illustrated by Victoria Chess.
        p.   cm.
Summary: After choosing a husband for his sweet singing voice,
a beautiful butterfly mourns the fact that he is swallowed by a
fish, until a king in his underwear reunites the two.
        ISBN 0-395-90015-8
[1. Folklore—Spain.] I. Chess, Victoria, ill. II. Title.
PZ8.1.S573Bg   2000
398.2'0946'045789—dc21
[E]   99-16616
                          CIP

TWP   10 9 8 7 6 5 4 3 2 1

For Gina −J. S.

To Elizabeth and Pirie, with love −V. C.

$\mathcal{I}$n Spain, once upon a time, there lived a beautiful
butterfly. Her delicate wings were flecked with the colors
of spring flowers, and she had the most enchanting dark
eyes. Everyone loved her.

One day as she was fluttering about, the butterfly found a little hollow in a tree. "What a perfect house for me," she thought. She swept away the dry leaves and cobwebs, and furnished her new home in the latest fashion. Then she sat on the balcony and let her wings wave beguilingly in the breeze.

Up the tree trunk hopped a cricket.

"Dear butterfly," he chirped. "You look partic-tic-tic-ularly lovely today. Tell me, will you marry me?"

"Perhaps," replied the butterfly. "And if I do marry you, how will you sing to our babies?"

The cricket rubbed his legs together smartly,

click-click!

click-click!

click-click!

"No, no!" scolded the butterfly. "Your lullaby would keep
the babies awake all night long! I cannot marry you."

Up climbed a green tree frog.

"Marry me, marry me," he croaked.

"Perhaps I will," said the butterfly. "And if I do marry you, how will you sing to our babies?"

The tree frog puffed out his throat and sang,

Croo-AH!
Croo-AH!
Croo-AH!

"Goodness gracious!" gasped the butterfly. "Your lullaby would frighten the babies! No, I could never marry you."

A little gray mouse tiptoed across a branch.

"Loveliest of butterflies," he whispered. "I would be so delighted if you would marry me."

"Perhaps I will marry you," said the butterfly. "And if I do, how will you sing to our babies?"

The mouse sang in a sweet small voice,

ee-ee-ee-ee-ee-ee-ee-ee-ee

"Marvelous," sighed the butterfly. "Our babies will *love* your lullaby. Yes, I will marry you."

The little mouse moved his belongings into the hollow tree, and the butterfly was so happy that she decided to make a honeymoon soup with sugar and rose petals. She gave her husband a bucket and asked him to fetch water for her.

The little mouse knelt beside the pond, holding the bucket with both paws. But the bucket was so heavy that he lost his balance and tumbled down, down, down . . .

Gulp! A fish snapped him up in one bite.

The butterfly waited an hour; she waited two hours.
Then a dove flew to the hollow tree and related the mouse's
sad fate.

The butterfly put on a black dress and a long black veil.
She flew to the bank of the pond and sat and wept. The dove,
because she was a good friend of the butterfly, perched above
her on a tree branch and called mournfully, *coo, coo.*

"Why are you calling *coo, coo?*" the tree asked.

"The little mouse fell in the water, and the butterfly is crying," replied the dove. "That is why I am calling *coo, coo.*"

"I am a good friend of the butterfly," said the tree, "so I will drop my leaves." The leaves drifted down into the pond.

"Why do you drop your leaves?" the pond asked.

"The little mouse fell in the water," the tree answered. "And the butterfly is crying, and the dove calls *coo, coo,* and so I drop my leaves."

"I am a good friend of the butterfly," said the pond, "so I will dry up," and it sank lower and lower in its banks.

The queen came to fetch water, but now the pond was
not much more than a mud puddle.

"Why have you dried up?" the queen asked the pond.

"The little mouse fell in the water, and the butterfly is
crying, and the dove calls *coo, coo,* and the tree drops its
leaves, so I have dried up," said the pond.

"I am a good friend of the butterfly," said the queen,
"so I will smash my water jars."

Along came her husband, the king. "Why are you
smashing your water jars?" he asked.

"The little mouse fell in the water, and the butterfly is crying, and the dove calls *coo, coo,* and the tree drops its leaves, and the pond has dried up, so I am smashing my water jars."

"I am a good friend of the butterfly," said the king, "and to show how sad I am, I will take off my robe and run around in my royal underwear."

Everyone had to laugh in spite of their sorrow. Even the
fish chuckled, *glu, glu, glu.* He opened his mouth and gave a
loud guffaw, and out tumbled the little mouse, good as new.
He ran to embrace his beloved butterfly.

Then the butterfly stopped crying, and the dove stopped calling *coo, coo,* and the tree stopped dropping its leaves, and the pond filled with water, and the queen stopped smashing her water jars, and the king put on his royal robe.

The beautiful butterfly and the little gray mouse lived happily in the hollow tree. They raised a family of little buttermice, and every night the mouse sang to them in a voice that was so soft and sweet,

ee-ee-ee-ee-ee-ee-ee-ee-ee.

FOLKLORE NOTE

Hundreds of variants of this folktale have been collected in Europe and Latin America. In Spanish-speaking areas, the heroine is always an insect—a flea, a cockroach, an ant, or a butterfly. The species of her suitors vary so widely that it seems this part of the tale is at the whim of each individual storyteller, except that the winner of the singing contest is almost always a mouse. The tale ends tragically when the poor husband either is eaten by a predator or drowns in a pot of soup, and all of nature joins the bride in mourning.

In telling this tale, I found that most children objected to the tragic ending, and so I was intrigued when I found variants from Castile and León in which a king runs around in his underwear. Suppose this episode brought about a happy ending. Certainly the king would make everyone laugh, including the cat or fish that had swallowed the mouse. I have taken the storyteller's liberty of making this change, and young listeners like it very much.

Though they often appear together, the two segments of this tale are classified separately by folklorists as Type 2023, *The Ant Who Married a Mouse,* and Type 2022, *An Animal Mourns the Death of a Spouse.*